W9-BKO-980

PAPA GATTO

An Italian Fairy Tale

Retold and Illustrated by RUTH SANDERSON

Little, Brown and Company
Boston New York Toronto London

Papa Gatto is based on various versions of an original Italian fairy tale, including: "The Colony of Cats" from *The Crimson Fairy Book,* by Andrew Lang (New York: McKay, 1903, 1947); "The Fable of the Cats" from *Italian Fables,* by Italo Calvino (New York: Orion, 1959); "The House of Cats" from *The House of Cats and Other Stories,* by John Hampden (New York: Farrar, Straus & Giroux, 1966); and "Count Gatto" from *Catlore: Tales from Around the World,* by Marjory Zaum (New York: Atheneum, 1985).

First Edition

Library of Congress Cataloging-in-Publication Data

Sanderson, Ruth.

Papa Gatto : an Italian fairy tale / retold and illustrated by Ruth Sanderson. — 1st ed.

p. cm.

Summary: Seeking someone to care for his motherless kittens, Papa Gatto, adviser to the prince, hires a beautiful but lazy girl, and then her plain but loving stepsister.

ISBN 0-316-77073-6

[1. Fairy tales. 2. Folklore — Italy.] I. Title.

PZ8.S253Pa 1995

398.2'09450452974428 — dc20

[E] 94-16725

10 9 8 7 6 5 4 3 2 1

NIL

Printed in Italy

The paintings for this book were done in Winsor & Newton oils on Giverney canvas paper.

This one is for Whitney

Long ago, in a time when it was not unusual for animals to speak, there lived a very clever cat. His great wisdom had earned him a position as the prince's adviser. Always trustworthy and kind to his fellow townspeople, the cat came to be known as Papa Gatto.

Papa Gatto lived with his wife in a fine mansion with a beautiful garden. Together they cared for their home, and together they prepared the nursery they hoped to fill with children. And sure enough, soon after the last pillow had been nestled into the big basket, eight kittens were born.

But Papa Gatto's joy had barely begun when his wife took ill and died. Grief-stricken, he knew he needed help caring for his babies. Because of his important position, Papa Gatto traveled throughout the kingdom and often could not be home. So he prepared an advertisement for the town crier to deliver on his daily rounds:

Helper needed to cook and to clean
For eight little kittens, already weaned.
You choose your payment, no amount too great.
Please see Papa Gatto before it's too late.

Now, in this same town there lived a widow with a daughter, Sophia, and a stepdaughter, Beatrice. Sophia was just like the widow: lovely to look at but lazy and coldhearted. Beatrice was much plainer than Sophia, but kind and hardworking. Yet the widow doted on Sophia, while Beatrice was ordered to tend the house and garden.

One day when Beatrice was weeding the garden, the three heard Papa Gatto's advertisement. Beatrice's heart went out to the little kittens whom she knew to be motherless. But when she expressed her desire to apply for the work, the widow laughed.

" 'You choose your payment, no amount too great'!" she cried. "If we were to trust you to choose, you would likely come home with empty pockets! No, I think Sophia is the one for this task."

Sophia, shocked at the idea of work, protested that she sneezed every time she even thought of kittens. But the widow insisted that she put on her best dress and sent her off to the mansion.

Sophia's protests were silenced by her greed when she saw Papa Gatto's beautiful home.

As for Papa Gatto, he was dazzled by Sophia's beauty.

Surely such a lovely person has a caring heart, he said to himself. And as he led her through the mansion to the nursery, where the kittens were waking from their nap, he took her silence for sympathy.

"May I ask if you can cook for kittens and keep a tidy house?" he asked. A dimpled smile was Sophia's only reply. "In that case, I hope you will start right away, for the prince requires my presence for a number of weeks."

The next day, Sophia gleefully watched Papa Gatto ride out of sight. Then she began to explore his home. She peered into all the cabinets and behind all the doors. She lifted every lid and opened every drawer. Then, in the room that had once belonged to Papa Gatto's beloved wife, she found the treasure she had been seeking.

Inside a carved jewelry box lay a necklace of eight sparkling diamonds. Papa Gatto had given the necklace to his wife on the day their eight kittens were born. Sophia decided that these diamonds would be her payment. As the strand was too small for her neck, she clasped it about her wrist.

But foolish Sophia did not know how to keep house or care for kittens — nor did she wish to learn. For weeks, the diamond necklace gleamed upon Sophia's wrist while the mansion turned dull with grime. Dirty dishes piled up everywhere. Heaps of dust collected in the corners, and cobwebs hung from the ceilings. The kittens' bedding was not washed or changed. Weeds choked the flowers in the garden.

When at last Papa Gatto returned, he could scarcely believe his eyes.

"What have you done to my home, you lazy girl?" he cried. Then he spied the diamond necklace on her wrist. With a yowl, he snatched it from her, leaving four long scratches in its place.

Then he spat, "Leave my house at once!"

"What about my payment?" exclaimed Sophia.

The angry cat bared his claws and said, "I'll gladly give you what you deserve — unless you leave this house at once!" And so Sophia fled.

Papa Gatto spent many days cleaning the mess Sophia had left behind. Then the prince sent word that he needed his adviser again. There was nothing Papa Gatto could do but send the town crier around the streets with another advertisement. But this time it said:

Can you provide kittens with care and with love,
And keep a house clean to the touch of a glove?
Papa Gatto's kittens must be happy and healthy,
And if his house gleams, you will leave there quite wealthy.

Once again, Beatrice heard the town crier. But this time, rather than tell her stepmother and stepsister of this second message, she quietly left for the mansion on her own.

As soon as Beatrice entered the nursery, Papa Gatto knew he had found someone he could trust. She tenderly stroked each kitten and murmured gentle words in soft tones. Yet her rough hands and plain clothes spoke of her familiarity with hard work. He left for his travels feeling confident that his babies and his home would be well cared for in his absence.

Each day, Beatrice fed the kittens carefully prepared dishes of tender meats and delicate fish. They frolicked in the sunshine while she tended the gardens. And each night, after she had tucked them into their basket, she cleaned the house from top to bottom.

The weeks passed, and the eight kittens grew to love Beatrice. They scampered about her in frisky abandon. Beatrice had never been happier in her life. Though she knew the widow and Sophia would never let her stay, she longed to remain at Papa Gatto's forever.

One day when the kittens and Beatrice were playing in the garden, Papa Gatto returned. His children saw him at the gate and ran to greet him with tails up and eyes bright.

"Are these my children, so happy and healthy?" Papa Gatto exclaimed. He entered the house and was pleased by what he saw. "And is this my home, so clean and tidy? You have more than earned your payment, my dear girl. Choose what you will from among my treasures."

Beatrice lowered her eyes. "I wish for nothing but your kind words," she said quietly. "For you see, it was my stepsister, Sophia, who caused you so much trouble. I choose only to right her wrong."

Papa Gatto looked at her in surprise. "Your stepsister's carelessness has nothing to do with you," he said kindly. "You have taken care of my home and my children. For this and for your honesty, I insist you have something to remember us by." And from his pocket, he removed the eight-diamond necklace and fastened it about Beatrice's wrist.

Beatrice was grateful for Papa Gatto's generosity, but the necklace did little to soothe her sad heart. She knew she would miss the kittens dreadfully. The tears in her eyes shone more brightly than the diamonds when she kissed them each good night and tucked them into bed one last time.

She left early the next morning before the kittens awoke.

When Beatrice returned home, she found the house strewn with dirty dishes and carelessly discarded clothing. The garden was full of weeds. But worse than this, she was confronted by the furious faces of Sophia and the widow as they returned from their morning stroll.

"A pretty mess you left us in these past weeks!" Sophia cried. "Where have you been?" Then she saw the diamonds — and understood her stepsister's absence. With one quick movement, she swept the jewels from Beatrice's wrist.

"I'll take this in payment for the scars that horrid cat left on my arm — and for my troubles while you were gone," she said spitefully.

Beatrice was angry, but she remained silent. More than ever, she longed to be back at Papa Gatto's home, for she loved the kittens and the quiet of the garden.

A few days later, the prince paid a visit to his adviser. "How happy your children are!" he exclaimed. Papa Gatto bowed, then related the tale of the two sisters. The prince's anger at Sophia's neglect turned to delight at Beatrice's kindness.

"Beatrice seems a remarkable girl," said the prince. Papa Gatto stroked his whiskers and smiled. He knew the prince had been seeking a wife.

"I have yet to know a kinder, more loving young woman," the wise cat said slyly. "I am sure Beatrice will be at the town fair tomorrow, wearing the diamonds I gave her. If you see her, please let her know we would welcome a visit."

"Indeed I will," replied the prince thoughtfully.

The streets of the town were gaily decorated the next day. Sophia and the widow were dressed in their finest gowns, and the diamonds twinkled on Sophia's wrist. Beatrice remained at home.

Suddenly the crowd parted. The prince strode toward the two ladies. He bowed deeply and said to Sophia, "Papa Gatto gave you these diamonds, did he not? You are the girl who cared for his kittens?"

Sophia realized he thought she was Beatrice. But she had heard the prince was in search of a wife, so rather than correct his mistake, she smiled prettily and replied, "Yes, I am the one who stayed at Papa Gatto's house."

The prince was enchanted by Sophia's beauty and soft voice. "Papa Gatto asks that you pay him and his dear children a visit," he said. "They miss you and wish to know that you are well. If you like, I would be happy to accompany you there myself."

Sophia thought quickly. Taking the widow's arm, she said, "I would gladly visit Papa Gatto's sweet kittens today, but I must help my poor mother home. You can see she is tired."

The prince smiled. "Ah, Beatrice, you are every bit as kind and caring as Papa Gatto said you were."

The prince watched the pair depart the festival, then returned to Papa Gatto's house full of happiness. He announced his desire to wed Beatrice as soon as possible. Papa Gatto and his kittens were overjoyed for their friend. But when the prince went on to praise Beatrice's golden hair and soft hands, Papa Gatto realized that the young man had been tricked.

The prince was astonished when Papa Gatto told him the truth.

"Lie to me, did she!" he cried. "She'll not get away with this. I shall go to her cottage this instant."

Papa Gatto insisted on joining the prince. He bundled up the kittens in a basket and set off with him to the widow's house.

When Sophia saw them approaching, she ran to Beatrice. "Give me your rags to wear and a veil to cover my face! Then stay out in the garden until I say you may come in!"

Beatrice was mystified by Sophia's strange behavior but exchanged clothes with her. Moments later, the prince and Papa Gatto knocked on the cottage door. The widow set the guests' basket on the table and called to Beatrice. Sophia, heavily veiled and wearing Beatrice's dress as well as the diamond bracelet, took the empty seat at the table.

"Beatrice, remove the veil so that I may see your lovely face," said the prince.

"Yes, Beatrice, if that is you, do not hide your honest face from us," said Papa Gatto.

Crafty Sophia shook her head and replied, "I have just now suffered a bad burn on my cheek from the heat of the stove. I must keep it covered for it to heal." The prince and Papa Gatto did not know what to do. Was this the true Beatrice or not?

Then Papa Gatto spied the bracelet gleaming on her wrist. And just below it, he saw four scars that matched his claws perfectly. With a yowl, he pounced and whisked the veil off Sophia's head. But instead of Sophia's beauty, the prince now saw only her ugly nature.

Then, before anyone could say anything, the top of the basket burst open and the eight kittens clambered out. They ignored Sophia and the widow, tumbling out the window into the garden, where Beatrice sat. With happy mews and purrs of contentment, they crawled into her arms and snuggled into the crook of her neck.

The prince and Papa Gatto rushed out to the garden. The prince knelt beside Beatrice and, taking her hand, asked her to marry him.

Beatrice looked him in the eye and replied, "You are known to be a kind and generous man, but I cannot marry you. I do not know you and so cannot yet love you. For too long I have lived in a house without love; I would not exchange one joyless home for another."

Then she looked at Papa Gatto. "There is only one place I have known happiness."

Papa Gatto smiled widely. "Then by all means, you must return to that place at once. My children have been pining for you. And perhaps the prince will agree to visit us often so that you may get to know him as I do."

The prince nodded happily, for he knew he would do all in his power to win the one whose beauty shone from within.

As for Sophia and the widow, they were left behind in the cottage, with no one to cook and clean and tend the garden but themselves.